SPLIT LOVE

A Journey Through Conflicting Emotions,

Uncertain Hearts,

and Embracing New Beginnings"

ISHMAEKUVOR

Introduction

Welcome to the captivating world of "Slip Love," a lesser-known facet of romantic connections where the heart dances between affection and hesitation, leaving those involved in a tender tug of war with their emotions. In this book, we explore the profound connection that lies beneath the surface of relationships, where love's transient nature dances in harmony with emotional struggles, leaving hearts suspended in a momentary serenade.

Through captivating narratives, real-life experiences, and psychological insights, we unravel the complexities of this emotional journey, providing guidance to those navigating its enigmatic path. Together, we encounter the signs of Slip Love, learn coping mechanisms to weather its storm, and find guidance in making decisions that can shape the course of our relationships.

This book serves as a tribute to the transient beauty of love and the strength of the human spirit in confronting the uncertainties that arise within it. As we embrace the intricacies of the human heart, let us find solace in the knowledge that we are not alone in navigating the depths of emotion. Together, we shall discover the transformative power of Slip Love and the wisdom it bestows upon us as we continue our pursuit of love, growth, and self-discovery.

"Slip Love":

TABLE OF CONTENTS

1. Introduction
  1.1 What is Slip Love?
  1.2 Understanding the Concept
  1.3 The Complexity of Emotions

2. Signs of Slip Love
  2.1 Recognizing Conflicting Emotions
    2.2 Identifying Uncertainty in a Relationship
  2.3 Analyzing Communication Patterns

3. Coping with Slip Love
    3.1 Self-Reflection and Emotional Awareness
  3.2 Seeking Support from Friends and Family
    3.3 Professional Counseling and Therapy

4. Making Decisions

4.1 Evaluating Relationship Compatibility

4.2 Weighing the Pros and Cons

4.3 Considering the Long-Term Impact

5. Communicating with Your Partner

5.1 Expressing Your Feelings Honestly

5.2 Encouraging Open Dialogue

5.3 Navigating Difficult Conversations

6. Taking Action

6.1 Deciding to Stay in the Relationship

6.2 Deciding to End the Relationship

6.3 Handling a Temporary Break

7. Moving Forward

7.1 Healing and Self-Care

7.2 Learning from the Experience

7.3 Embracing New Beginnings

8. Conclusion

8.1 Embracing the Journey of Love

: **Introduction**

1.1 What is Slip Love? Understanding the Tug of Emotions

In this section, we delve into the intricacies of Slip Love, exploring its essence and what sets it apart from regular romantic connections. Slip Love refers to the bittersweet experience of being in a relationship while feeling uncertain or conflicted about one's emotions. We explore the delicate balance between love and doubt, highlighting how it can manifest in different ways for individuals.

We'll examine common scenarios that lead to Slip Love, such as emotional distance, differing life goals, or unresolved past experiences. By understanding these factors, readers can gain insight into their own relationships and recognize the signs of Slip Love when they arise.

1.2 Unraveling the Complexity of Slip Love

This subsection delves deeper into the complex nature of Slip Love, shedding light on the emotional and psychological dynamics that make it so challenging to navigate. We explore the internal struggle experienced by individuals caught in the web of Slip Love, where love and uncertainty intertwine, leaving hearts torn between two conflicting paths.

Through real-life examples and psychological insights, we help readers understand why Slip Love can be both captivating and heart-wrenching. We discuss the emotional toll it takes on individuals, emphasizing the importance of self-compassion and seeking support during such turbulent times.

1.3   Navigating the Rollercoaster of Slip Love

This part of the introduction focuses on the emotional journey that characterizes Slip Love. We discuss the rollercoaster of emotions experienced by those involved, including joy, doubt, hope, and fear. We'll address the emotional highs and lows that make Slip Love feel like an unpredictable ride, exploring how such fluctuations can impact relationships and personal well-being.

By offering coping strategies and tips for emotional resilience, readers can better navigate the challenging emotional landscape of Slip Love. We discuss the significance of effective communication, introspection, and seeking professional guidance when needed, empowering readers to embrace their emotions and make informed decisions.

Overall, the introduction sets the stage for a heartfelt exploration of Slip Love, providing readers with a compassionate and insightful guide to understand and manage this unique emotional experience. It serves as a foundation for the subsequent chapters, where we delve deeper into the signs, coping mechanisms, decision-making, and healing processes related to Slip Love.

Content 2: Signs of Slip Love

2.1 Conflicting Emotions: The Telltale Signs of Slip Love

In this section, we delve into the heart of Slip Love, exploring the signs that distinguish it from regular affectionate feelings. We discuss the emotional conflict that arises when love intertwines with doubt, leaving individuals torn between the euphoria of being in love and the unease of uncertainty. Readers will learn to recognize the emotional rollercoaster unique to Slip Love, such as experiencing moments of joy followed by waves of doubt, fear, or anxiety.

We emphasize the importance of introspection and emotional awareness to identify the presence of Slip Love in their relationships. By understanding the inner turmoil and mixed feelings that often accompany this experience, readers can begin to navigate their emotions with more clarity and compassion.

2.2 Uncertainty in Love: Recognizing Slip Love in Relationships

This subsection delves deeper into the uncertainty that clouds the perception of love in a relationship. We explore how Slip Love can manifest in different ways, such as feeling disconnected from one's partner despite genuine affection or questioning the long-term compatibility of the relationship. Readers will gain insights into how external factors, unresolved past experiences, or unmet expectations can contribute to feelings of uncertainty in a romantic connection.

Through relatable anecdotes and expert insights, readers will discover that experiencing uncertainty in love is a natural part of relationships and doesn't necessarily diminish the depth of feelings. Instead, it provides an opportunity for growth and understanding as individuals confront their emotions with openness and vulnerability.

2.3 Unspoken Words: Communication Patterns in Slip Love

Effective communication is a cornerstone of any successful relationship, but it becomes even more critical in the context of Slip Love. In this part, we examine how Slip Love can influence communication patterns between partners. We explore scenarios where individuals might struggle to express their emotions honestly due to fear of judgment or the risk of disrupting the relationship.

Readers will gain valuable strategies for fostering open dialogue in Slip Love situations. We encourage the importance of sharing feelings, uncertainties, and desires with one's partner, creating an environment where both individuals feel heard and understood. By developing effective communication skills, individuals can navigate Slip Love with greater empathy and mutual support.

Overall, this section serves as a comprehensive guide to recognizing the signs of Slip Love and understanding the complex emotions that underpin this experience. Armed with this knowledge, readers can take the first steps towards embracing the intricacies of Slip Love and finding a path to emotional growth and resolution in their relationships.

Content 3: Coping with Slip Love

Navigating Slip Love can be an emotionally challenging journey, as it requires individuals to confront conflicting emotions and uncertainties within themselves and their relationships. In this section, we delve into the coping mechanisms and strategies that can help individuals navigate the complex terrain of Slip Love and find emotional healing and growth.

3.1 Self-Reflection and Emotional Awareness in Slip Love

Self-reflection is a powerful tool in any emotional journey, and it becomes especially crucial when dealing with Slip Love. In this subsection, we explore the significance of self-awareness and emotional intelligence in understanding the root causes of conflicting emotions.

Readers will be encouraged to delve deep within themselves, asking questions about their fears, desires, and expectations in the relationship. By uncovering and acknowledging these feelings, individuals can gain clarity about their emotional state and the reasons behind their uncertainties.

We also introduce techniques for developing emotional awareness, such as journaling, meditation, and mindfulness exercises. These practices can help individuals attune to their emotions and recognize patterns of thought and behavior that may contribute to Slip Love.

By fostering self-reflection and emotional awareness, individuals can approach Slip Love with a sense of compassion towards themselves and their partners. It provides an opportunity for self-acceptance and growth, allowing them to embrace their vulnerabilities and explore the depths of their emotions without judgment.

3.2 Seeking Support: Overcoming Slip Love Together

Slip Love can be a lonely and isolating experience, but it doesn't have to be. In this part, we highlight the importance of seeking support from friends, family, or support groups. We emphasize that individuals going through Slip Love are not alone in their struggles, and sharing their experiences can bring a sense of relief and understanding.

We explore the power of open conversations with trusted confidants, allowing individuals to express their feelings and concerns without fear of judgment. Moreover, seeking support can provide different perspectives and insights that may shed light on potential solutions or paths forward.

Additionally, we discuss the significance of seeking professional help from counselors or therapists specialized in relationship dynamics and emotional struggles. Professional guidance can offer a safe and confidential space for individuals to explore their emotions and gain practical coping strategies.

By building a support network, individuals can find comfort in knowing they have a community that empathizes with their journey and supports them through the ups and downs of Slip Love. This sense of solidarity can be instrumental in providing the emotional strength needed to navigate the complexities of Slip Love.

3.3 Healing Hearts: The Role of Professional Help in Slip Love

In this subsection, we dive deeper into the role of professional counseling and therapy in healing hearts wounded by Slip Love. We explore the benefits of seeking professional help in managing conflicting emotions and uncertainties, and how therapy can be a transformative experience.

Therapy provides a non-judgmental space for individuals to explore their emotions, gain self-awareness, and develop coping strategies. A skilled therapist can guide individuals through the process of healing and growth, empowering them to make informed decisions and overcome emotional obstacles.

We shed light on various therapeutic approaches that have proven effective in helping individuals navigate Slip Love, such as cognitive-behavioral therapy (CBT), emotion-focused therapy, or couples counseling.

Moreover, we address any potential hesitations or stigmas that individuals may have about seeking professional help. We emphasize that therapy is not a sign of weakness but rather a courageous step towards personal growth and emotional well-being.

By embracing professional help, individuals can embark on a journey of self-discovery and emotional healing, gaining the tools to confront Slip Love with resilience and compassion.

In conclusion, this section explores the coping mechanisms and support systems that can aid individuals in navigating the emotional challenges of Slip Love. By fostering self-reflection, seeking support from loved ones, and embracing professional guidance, readers can find the strength to confront their emotions and make informed decisions about their relationships. Coping with Slip Love is a transformative process that can lead to profound personal growth, offering the opportunity for individuals to emerge from this emotional symphony with greater self-awareness and resilience.

Content 4: Making Decisions

Making decisions in the context of Slip Love can be a daunting task, as conflicting emotions and uncertainties cloud the path forward. In this section, we explore the essential considerations and thought processes involved in determining the fate of a relationship affected by Slip Love.

4.1 Compatibility Check: Deciding the Future of Slip Love

The foundation of any successful relationship is compatibility – a shared understanding of values, goals, and priorities. In this subsection, we delve into the importance of assessing the compatibility of partners when confronted with Slip Love.

Readers will be guided through a series of self-reflection exercises and conversations with their partners to evaluate how aligned they are in their long-term visions for the relationship. We discuss the significance of discussing core values, life goals, and desired levels of commitment to gauge whether the relationship can withstand the challenges posed by Slip Love.

We also encourage readers to consider the elements that initially drew them together and whether those aspects still hold true in the present. By examining compatibility, individuals can gain clarity about the future of their relationship and whether it has the potential to weather the storm of Slip Love.

4.2 Weighing the Pros and Cons: Choices in Slip Love

When faced with Slip Love, individuals may feel torn between staying in the relationship and exploring new paths. In this part, we guide readers through the process of weighing the pros and cons of each choice.

We encourage individuals to create a list of the positive aspects of the relationship, the reasons they fell in love, and the unique bond they share with their partner. On the other side, we explore the challenges and uncertainties that come with Slip Love, including potential emotional distress or the fear of making the wrong decision.

By carefully examining the pros and cons, readers can gain a clearer understanding of their priorities and feelings, enabling them to make more informed decisions about the future of their relationship.

4.3 Long-Term Impact: The Ripple Effects of Slip Love Decisions

In this subsection, we discuss the long-term implications of the decisions individuals make in the context of Slip Love. Whether they choose to stay in the relationship or part ways, there will be consequences that extend beyond the present moment.

We explore the potential outcomes of each decision, including the impact on individual growth, emotional well-being, and future relationships. Readers will be encouraged to contemplate how their choices in Slip Love can shape their lives and the lives of those around them.

Moreover, we discuss the significance of communicating openly with their partner about their decision-making process. Honest and compassionate dialogue can foster understanding and provide closure, regardless of the outcome.

By considering the long-term impact of their decisions, individuals can approach Slip Love with a sense of responsibility and foresight, ultimately choosing a path that aligns with their values and aspirations.

In conclusion, this section offers a comprehensive guide to making decisions in the context of Slip Love. By assessing compatibility, weighing the pros and cons, and contemplating the long-term impact, individuals can gain the clarity and confidence needed to move forward in their relationships with resilience and authenticity.

Every decision made in Slip Love is an opportunity for growth and self-discovery, and readers will find that by embracing the complexities of this emotional journey, they can emerge stronger and wiser, regardless of the choices they make.

Content 5: Communicating with Your Partner

Effective communication is the lifeline of any relationship, and in the context of Slip Love, it becomes paramount. In this section, we embark on a comprehensive exploration of communication strategies that can strengthen the emotional bond between partners and foster mutual understanding in the face of uncertainty.

5.1 Honesty in Slip Love: Expressing Feelings without Hesitation

Honesty is the bedrock of open and authentic communication. In this subsection, we delve into the importance of being honest with oneself and one's partner about feelings, doubts, and uncertainties in Slip Love.

We guide readers through the process of acknowledging and embracing their emotions, no matter how challenging they may be. By expressing feelings without hesitation, individuals can create a safe space for their partners to do the same, nurturing a deeper emotional connection.

We provide practical tips on how to initiate honest conversations with their partners, such as finding the right time and place to talk and using "I" statements to express emotions without placing blame. Honesty in Slip Love lays the groundwork for open communication, allowing both partners to feel seen, heard, and supported.

5.2 Embracing Dialogue: Strengthening Bonds in Slip Love

In this part, we explore the art of embracing dialogue in the midst of Slip Love's emotional turbulence. Effective communication involves not only expressing one's feelings but also actively listening to one's partner's perspective.

We introduce active listening techniques that promote empathy and understanding, such as reflective listening and validation of emotions. By acknowledging each other's feelings without judgment, partners can foster a deep sense of emotional connection and validation.

Moreover, we discuss the significance of asking open-ended questions to encourage deeper conversations. By inviting their partners to share their thoughts and emotions, individuals can gain valuable insights into their partner's perspective and emotional state.

Through embracing dialogue, individuals can create a communication dynamic that transcends Slip Love's challenges, fostering a foundation of trust and emotional intimacy.

5.3 Navigating Difficult Conversations in Slip Love

In this subsection, we explore the inevitable challenges that arise in Slip Love conversations and provide guidance on how to navigate them with sensitivity and care.

We discuss common roadblocks in communication, such as defensiveness, blame-shifting, or avoiding difficult topics altogether. By recognizing these barriers, individuals can take proactive steps to foster a non-confrontational and compassionate environment for dialogue.

We offer practical strategies for navigating difficult conversations, such as using "I" statements to express feelings, seeking common ground, and taking breaks when emotions become overwhelming. These techniques can help keep the lines of communication open and productive, even in the face of emotional intensity.

Moreover, we discuss the importance of practicing self-compassion during challenging conversations. Slip Love can stir up feelings of vulnerability and insecurity, and it's essential to approach these conversations with gentleness towards oneself and one's partner.

By learning to navigate difficult conversations with emotional intelligence, individuals can lay the groundwork for deeper emotional connection and understanding, even in the midst of Slip Love's uncertainties.

In conclusion, this section offers a comprehensive guide to effective communication in the context of Slip Love. By embracing honesty, dialogue, and navigating difficult conversations with sensitivity, individuals can nurture a profound emotional bond with their partners.

Through open and compassionate communication, partners can confront the challenges of Slip Love together, fostering a sense of unity and resilience that can withstand the uncertainties of this emotional journey.

By recognizing the power of communication in fostering emotional connection and mutual understanding, readers will find that they can navigate Slip Love with greater emotional intelligence and create a relationship built on honesty, trust, and empathy.

Content 6: Taking Action

In the realm of Slip Love, decisions carry immense weight, as they shape the future of relationships and individuals' emotional well-being. In this section, we explore the various paths individuals can take when confronted with Slip Love and provide guidance on how to approach each decision with clarity, courage, and compassion.

6.1 Staying Steadfast: Commitment in Slip Love

For some individuals, the decision to stay in the relationship despite Slip Love's uncertainties may feel like an act of courage and determination. In this subsection, we delve into the concept of staying steadfast in Slip Love and the elements that contribute to making such a decision.

Readers will explore the importance of commitment and emotional investment in the relationship. We discuss the value of embracing the imperfections and uncertainties that come with Slip Love while maintaining the resolve to work through challenges together.

We explore the significance of focusing on the present moment and finding joy in the love that exists amidst the uncertainties. By staying committed to the relationship, individuals can cultivate a sense of stability and security, nurturing the emotional bond between partners.

Moreover, we discuss the role of communication and vulnerability in navigating Slip Love while staying steadfast. Honest conversations about one's feelings and uncertainties can create an environment of mutual support and understanding.

By exploring the elements that contribute to staying committed in Slip Love, individuals can approach their relationships with renewed dedication and a sense of purpose, finding strength in their emotional connection with their partners.

6.2 Farewell or Second Chance? Deciding the Fate of Slip Love

For others, the decision to end the relationship or take a break may be the path that aligns with their emotional journey. In this part, we explore the complexity of saying farewell to a relationship affected by Slip Love or choosing to take a temporary break to gain perspective.

Readers will be guided through a process of self-exploration and introspection to identify whether ending the relationship aligns with their core values and aspirations. We discuss the importance of listening to one's intuition and recognizing when a relationship is no longer serving one's emotional well-being.

In cases where individuals choose a temporary break, we explore the purpose of this period of separation and how it can lead to personal growth and clarity. We emphasize the significance of setting clear boundaries and communication during this time to avoid misunderstandings and maintain respect for each other's emotions.

Moreover, we discuss the emotional aftermath of making the decision to end the relationship or take a break. We offer guidance on coping with grief, loss, and navigating the process of healing and self-discovery.

By exploring the complexities of saying farewell or taking a break in Slip Love, individuals can approach these decisions with greater self-awareness and compassion for both themselves and their partners.

6.3 Temporary Break: A Pause in Slip Love's Journey

In this subsection, we delve deeper into the concept of taking a temporary break in Slip Love and the potential benefits of such a decision.

Readers will gain insights into the purpose of a temporary break – a time for reflection, personal growth, and gaining perspective on the relationship. We discuss how this break can provide individuals with the emotional space needed to understand their feelings and needs more clearly.

We explore the significance of setting boundaries and communication guidelines during the break to avoid miscommunication and emotional distress. Moreover, we discuss the role of ongoing support and counseling during this period to help individuals navigate their emotions and uncertainties.

By understanding the purpose and potential benefits of a temporary break, individuals can make an informed decision about taking this pause in Slip Love's journey, recognizing that it can be a step towards personal growth and clarity.

In conclusion, this section offers a comprehensive exploration of taking action in the context of Slip Love. By exploring the elements that contribute to staying committed, making the decision to say farewell or take a break, and understanding the purpose of a temporary break, readers will be equipped with the tools to approach their relationships with courage, authenticity, and compassion.

Taking action in Slip Love is an act of self-discovery and emotional resilience, and readers will find that by exploring these choices with introspection and vulnerability, they can navigate the complexities of their emotional journey with greater clarity and confidence.

Ultimately, individuals will be empowered to make decisions aligned with their values, aspirations, and emotional well-being, fostering a sense of empowerment and self-compassion as they continue their journey through Slip Love and beyond.

Content 7: Moving Forward

The journey through Slip Love is a transformative experience that leaves individuals changed in profound ways. In this section, we explore the healing process and the steps individuals can take to move forward with resilience, compassion, and newfound wisdom.

7.1 Healing Hearts: Self-Care and Recovery after Slip Love

Healing after Slip Love requires a delicate balance of self-compassion, self-care, and emotional support. In this subsection, we delve into the essential practices that can aid individuals in their journey of recovery and emotional well-being.

Readers will explore the significance of self-compassion in acknowledging and validating their emotions without self-judgment. We discuss the power of self-care practices, such as mindfulness, exercise, creative expression, and spending time with loved ones, to nourish the soul and foster emotional healing.

Moreover, we discuss the role of therapy and counseling in the healing process, providing individuals with a safe and supportive environment to explore their emotions and gain insights into their personal growth.

By embracing self-compassion and self-care, individuals can embark on a journey of healing, allowing themselves the time and space needed to mend their hearts and rediscover their emotional strength.

7.2 Lessons Learned: Growth and Transformation from Slip Love

In this part, we explore the valuable lessons that can be gleaned from the experience of Slip Love. Every emotional journey offers opportunities for growth and transformation, and Slip Love is no exception.

Readers will be guided through a process of introspection and reflection on the lessons they have learned throughout their Slip Love experience. We discuss the insights gained from exploring conflicting emotions, uncertainties, and vulnerabilities, as well as the newfound wisdom that emerges from embracing such complexities.

We also discuss the potential positive outcomes of Slip Love, such as enhanced emotional resilience, improved communication skills, and a deeper understanding of personal needs and desires.

By recognizing the growth and transformation that emerge from Slip Love, individuals can find solace in the knowledge that their emotional journey has not been in vain. Instead, they can view it as a stepping stone towards personal development and a deeper connection with themselves.

7.3 Embracing New Beginnings: The Road Beyond Slip Love

In this subsection, we explore the concept of embracing new beginnings after Slip Love. As individuals heal and grow from their experiences, they may find themselves ready to embark on a new chapter of their lives.

Readers will be encouraged to explore their hopes, dreams, and aspirations beyond Slip Love. We discuss the significance of setting new goals and intentions, fostering a sense of hope and excitement for the future.

We also explore the potential for new relationships or rekindling connections with past partners, emphasizing the importance of entering new chapters with open hearts and minds.

By embracing new beginnings, individuals can find a renewed sense of purpose and direction, leaving Slip Love's uncertainties in the past and stepping into a future filled with hope and possibility.

7.4 Moving Forward Together: Rebuilding Trust and Emotional Connection

For individuals who choose to stay in their relationship after Slip Love, rebuilding trust and emotional connection becomes a vital aspect of moving forward.

In this part, we explore the process of healing and rebuilding within the context of a relationship. We discuss the significance of open and honest communication about the Slip Love experience and the emotions that arose during that time.

We provide guidance on how to create a safe space for vulnerability and emotional expression, where partners can share their feelings and experiences without fear of judgment.

Moreover, we discuss the importance of forgiveness and empathy in the healing process. By acknowledging each other's pain and vulnerabilities, partners can foster a deep sense of emotional connection and trust.

By moving forward together, partners can embark on a new phase of their relationship, fortified by the shared experience of Slip Love and a commitment to nurturing a deeper emotional bond.

7.5 Embracing Emotional Resilience: Navigating Future Challenges

Emotional resilience is a valuable skill in navigating the challenges that arise in any relationship. In this part, we explore the concept of emotional resilience and its significance in the context of Slip Love.

Readers will learn practical strategies for cultivating emotional resilience, such as practicing mindfulness, developing healthy coping mechanisms, and fostering a positive outlook on life.

We discuss the importance of communication in maintaining emotional resilience, as open dialogue with partners can help address challenges before they become overwhelming.

Moreover, we explore the power of support networks in bolstering emotional resilience. Friends, family, or professional counselors can provide valuable insights and emotional support during difficult times.

By embracing emotional resilience, individuals can approach future challenges with greater courage and confidence, knowing they possess the strength to navigate the complexities of Slip Love and beyond.

In conclusion, this section offers a comprehensive exploration of moving forward after Slip Love. By embracing healing practices, learning from the experience, embracing new beginnings, rebuilding emotional connection, and fostering emotional resilience, individuals can find the strength and wisdom to navigate the complexities of Slip Love and emerge with a profound sense of growth and self-discovery.

Moving forward from Slip Love is a transformative journey of self-empowerment and emotional healing, and readers will find that by embracing these principles, they can navigate the uncertainties of their emotional journey with grace and resilience.

Content 8: Embracing Self-Discovery

In the aftermath of Slip Love, individuals often find themselves on a profound journey of self-discovery. In this section, we explore the transformative process of embracing self-discovery and gaining a deeper understanding of one's identity, desires, and purpose.

8.1 The Journey Within: Exploring Self-Identity

Self-discovery begins with an exploration of one's self-identity. In this subsection, we delve into the process of understanding who we are beyond the boundaries of relationships and societal expectations.

Readers will be guided through introspective exercises that delve into their values, passions, strengths, and unique qualities. We discuss the significance of self-awareness in recognizing patterns of behavior and thought that may have influenced their Slip Love experience.

By understanding their self-identity, individuals can lay the groundwork for a journey of authenticity and self-acceptance, embracing all aspects of themselves with compassion and understanding.

8.2 Embracing Vulnerability: The Gateway to Growth

Vulnerability is often viewed as a weakness, but in the journey of self-discovery, it becomes a powerful gateway to growth and emotional healing.

In this part, we explore the concept of vulnerability and its significance in uncovering deeper truths about ourselves. We discuss how embracing vulnerability allows us to confront our fears and insecurities, leading to a profound sense of self-acceptance.

Readers will be encouraged to step out of their comfort zones and lean into vulnerability, recognizing that it is through vulnerability that they can experience transformative growth and forge meaningful connections with others.

8.3 Aligning with Desires and Aspirations

In the pursuit of self-discovery, aligning with our desires and aspirations becomes essential. In this subsection, we explore the significance of understanding what truly brings us joy, fulfillment, and purpose.

Readers will be guided through exercises that help them identify their passions and dreams, and explore how they align with their current life choices.

We discuss the process of setting goals that align with their authentic selves, empowering them to make choices that lead to greater fulfillment and satisfaction.

8.4 Embracing Change: Letting Go and Moving Forward

Self-discovery often involves navigating change, which can be both liberating and challenging. In this part, we explore the process of letting go of old patterns, relationships, or beliefs that no longer serve our growth.

Readers will be encouraged to embrace change as an opportunity for renewal and self-reinvention. We discuss the power of resilience in navigating transitions and the importance of self-compassion in times of uncertainty.

By embracing change and letting go of what no longer serves them, individuals can create space for new opportunities and experiences that align with their authentic selves.

8.5 Cultivating Mindfulness: Being Present in the Journey

Mindfulness is a powerful tool in the journey of self-discovery. In this subsection, we delve into the practice of mindfulness and its significance in staying present and attuned to our inner experiences.

Readers will learn mindfulness techniques to cultivate a deeper sense of self-awareness and emotional regulation. We explore how mindfulness can help individuals navigate challenging emotions and thoughts, fostering a sense of inner peace and clarity.

By cultivating mindfulness, individuals can approach their journey of self-discovery with a sense of curiosity and openness, fully immersing themselves in the present moment.

8.6 Embracing Authenticity: Living Your Truth

Authenticity is at the core of self-discovery. In this part, we explore the concept of living one's truth and embracing authenticity in all aspects of life.

Readers will be encouraged to honor their true selves and make choices that align with their values and aspirations. We discuss the power of authenticity in building meaningful connections with others and finding a sense of purpose and fulfillment.

Moreover, we explore how authenticity can help individuals navigate future relationships and emotional challenges with greater clarity and resilience.

8.7 The Journey Continues: Self-Discovery as a Lifelong Process

In this subsection, we emphasize that self-discovery is a lifelong process, and Slip Love is just one chapter in the larger narrative of personal growth.

Readers will be encouraged to embrace the idea that self-discovery is an ongoing journey filled with opportunities for growth and transformation.

We discuss the importance of continued self-reflection, learning, and exploration, as it allows individuals to evolve and adapt as they navigate the complexities of life.

In conclusion, this section offers a comprehensive exploration of self-discovery after Slip Love. By understanding one's self-identity, embracing vulnerability, aligning with desires and aspirations, letting go, cultivating mindfulness, embracing authenticity, and recognizing self-discovery as a lifelong journey, individuals can find profound growth, self-acceptance, and purpose.

The journey of self-discovery is a gift that emerges from the depths of Slip Love, providing individuals with the tools to navigate future challenges and relationships with authenticity and resilience.

By embracing the transformative process of self-discovery, readers will find that they can navigate the uncertainties of Slip Love and emerge with a profound sense of self-empowerment, emotional wisdom, and a deeper connection with their authentic selves.

CONCLUSION

In the pages of "Ephemeral Serenade: Navigating the Symphony of Slip Love," we have explored the intricate dance of emotions that define Slip Love. The conflicting feelings, uncertainties, and vulnerabilities that intertwine in this symphony of love have been laid bare.

Throughout this journey, we have provided guidance on making decisions with clarity and compassion, whether it's staying steadfast, saying farewell, taking a break, or moving forward together. We emphasized the significance of effective communication and support in nurturing emotional bonds with partners.

The transformative process of self-discovery has been a focal point, as individuals embark on a profound journey of introspection and vulnerability. By embracing authenticity and mindfulness, they can navigate Slip Love with resilience and find self-acceptance and purpose.

Healing after Slip Love requires self-compassion, self-care, and emotional support. The power of therapy and counseling has been underscored as a safe space for emotional exploration and recovery.

As the final notes of this symphony sound, we hope readers leave with wisdom and solace, understanding that Slip Love is a transformative journey that touches the soul. The ebb and flow of emotions are a testament to the resilience of the human spirit.

In the transient beauty of love, let us find the courage to embrace vulnerability, navigate uncertainties, and embark on a journey of self-discovery. Together, we can navigate Slip Love, forging deeper connections and discovering the essence of being human.

With hearts open to the symphony of Slip Love, let us remember that the dance of emotions brings growth and understanding, guiding us to a deeper connection with ourselves and those we hold dear.

THE MORAL LESSON TO BE LEARN FROM SLIPT LOVE

Navigating the Symphony of Slip Love" is that love is a complex and transformative journey that requires courage, vulnerability, and self-discovery. The book emphasizes the following key moral lessons:

1. **Embracing Vulnerability:** The journey of love and relationships requires individuals to embrace vulnerability, acknowledging their emotions and uncertainties without fear or

shame. By leaning into vulnerability, we can forge deeper connections with ourselves and others, fostering a sense of authenticity and emotional intimacy.

2. **Effective Communication**: Open and honest communication is the lifeline of any relationship. By actively listening to our partners' perspectives and expressing our feelings with compassion, we can navigate the complexities of Slip Love with empathy and understanding.

3. **Self-Discovery and Growth**: Slip Love can be a catalyst for self-discovery and personal growth. By exploring our self-identity, desires, and aspirations, we can

align ourselves with authenticity and make choices that lead to greater fulfillment and purpose.

4. **Healing and Self-Care:** The journey of Slip Love may leave emotional wounds, and healing requires self-compassion and self-care. By seeking support, therapy, and taking time to nurture our emotional well-being, we can mend our hearts and find strength to move forward.

5. **Embracing Change:** Slip Love may lead us to make difficult decisions, such as staying committed or saying farewell. Embracing change and letting go of what no longer serves us can open doors to new opportunities and personal growth.

6. **Mindfulness and Resilience**: Cultivating mindfulness and emotional resilience empowers us to navigate Slip Love's uncertainties with grace and strength. Being present in the moment and approaching challenges with a positive outlook fosters emotional well-being.

7. **Authenticity and Living Our Truth:** Embracing authenticity allows us to honor our true selves, leading to deeper connections with others and a sense of purpose. By living our truth, we can forge meaningful relationships and make choices aligned with our values.

In conclusion, the moral lesson from "SLIPT LOVE"

Navigating the Symphony of Slip Love" is that love's journey is transformative, and navigating Slip Love requires courage, self-discovery, and emotional resilience. Embracing vulnerability, effective communication, and authenticity can lead to profound growth, healing, and a deeper connection with ourselves and our partners.